Great Beginnings
ACTIVITIES FOR GIFTED AND TALENTED KIDS

Hip, Hip, Hooray!
LANGUAGE ARTS ACTIVITIES

LEVEL 2

by Laurie Steding
illustrated by Wayne Becker

Watermill Press

Copyright © 1994 by Watermill Press, an imprint of Troll Associates, Inc. No part of this book may be used or reproduced in any manner whatsoever without written permission from the publisher.
Printed in the United States of America.

10 9 8 7 6 5 4 3

Dear Parents:

Congratulations for taking an important step that will help your child discover and develop his or her academic potential! As you explore the pages of this workbook with your child, you will find interesting and challenging activities that encourage thinking skills such as organizing information, logical reasoning, analyzing, and generating creativity.

All children need to memorize addition and subtraction facts, letter-sound relationships, sight words, and basic rules of grammar in their primary years of school. This workbook, while reinforcing many of those skills, is intended to provide the gifted child with extension activities that will encourage him or her to think logically and analytically.

Gifted children need guidance in their learning just as much as other children. They need to be allowed to experiment with problems that don't have simple right or wrong answers, but rather encourage different types of solutions. They need permission to be creative. And above all, they need to be accepted for what they are—ordinary kids with special thinking abilities. Both the open-ended activities and the problems with concrete answers will help to build self-confidence in your child.

We hope you enjoy this workbook as a tool to help you stay involved with your child's learning. Let your child set the pace for his or her learning. It should be stimulating and fun for both of you!

VISUAL DISCRIMINATION

Food Fun

Can you find all the food words hidden in this puzzle? Some of the words are listed below to help you find them. There are 4 other words hidden.

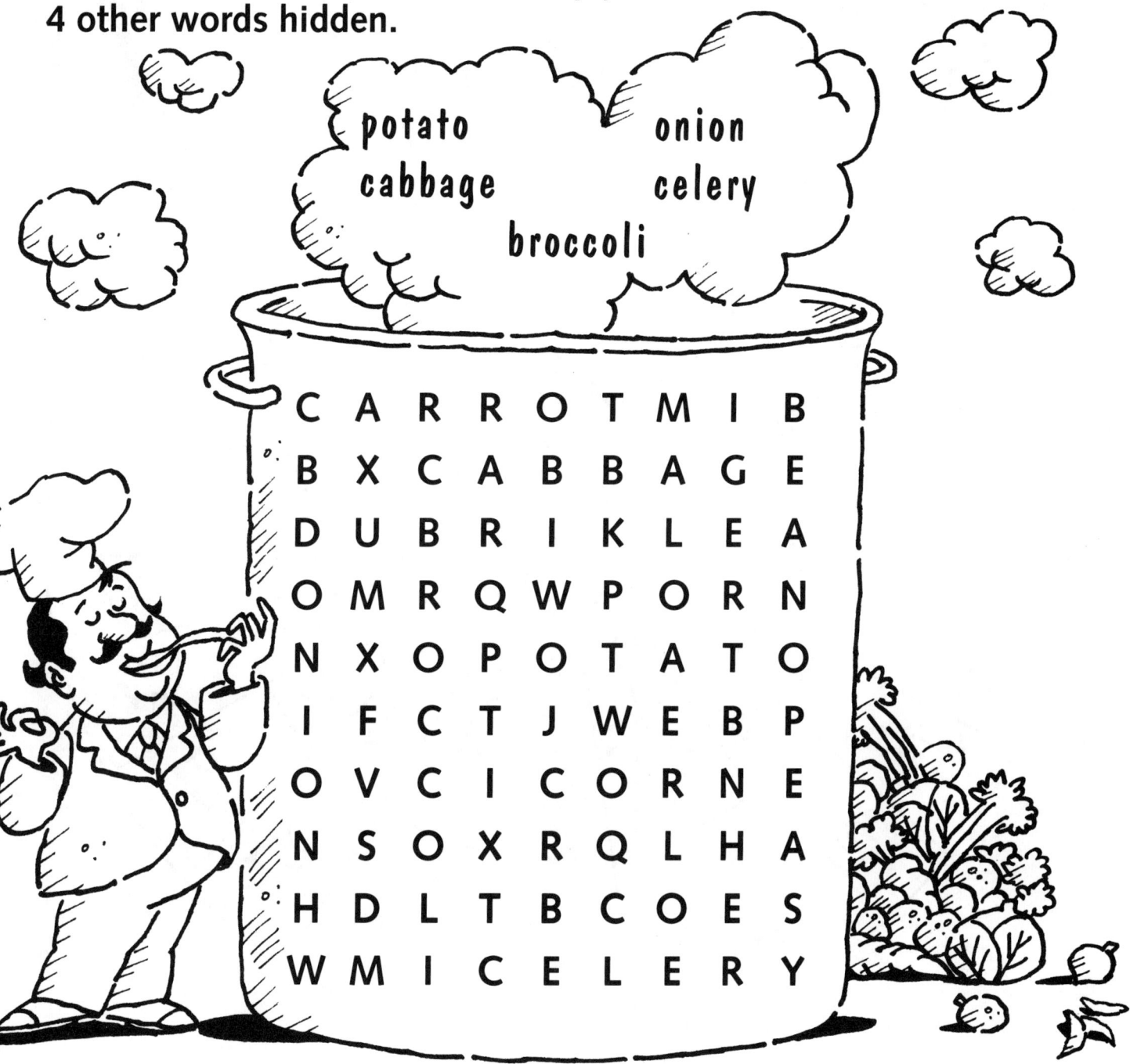

potato   onion
cabbage   celery
broccoli

```
C A R R O T M I B
B X C A B B A G E
D U B R I K L E A
O M R Q W P O R N
N X O P O T A T O
I F C T J W E B P
O V C I C O R N E
N S O X R Q L H A
H D L T B C O E S
W M I C E L E R Y
```

What do all these foods have in common?

DECODING/LETTER SKILLS

Crack the Code!

Use the decoding circle to help figure out the secret message below.

DECODING/LETTER SKILLS

Circus Caper

Use the decoding circle on page 4 to solve the riddle below.

LOGICAL REASONING

Design your own secret code. Fill in the decoding circle with your choice of shapes, letters, numbers, or any combinations you wish.

CREATIVE WRITING

The Secret Code Is . . .

Make up your own story or sentences. Write them in code using your decoding circle. Then ask someone else to decode your writing!

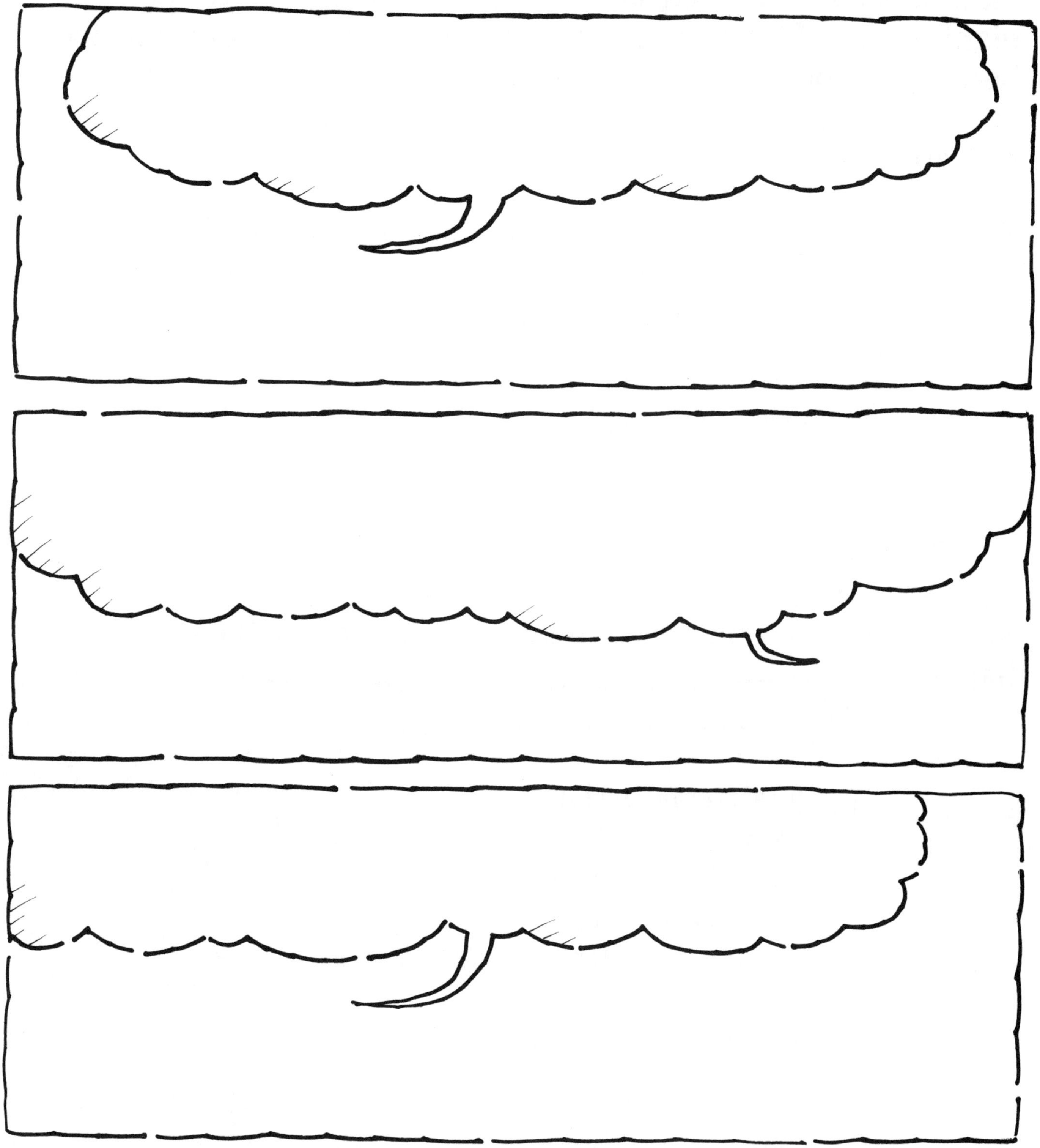

ATTRIBUTES/CLASSIFICATION/LOGICAL REASONING

The Picky Princess

Remember the fairy tale about the Princess and the Pea? The queen hid a tiny dried pea underneath a mattress, and piled dozens more mattresses on top. Then she invited a young maiden to spend the night on top of the mattresses. The young maiden could not sleep because the pea made her so uncomfortable. The queen decided the young maiden must be a real princess. And the prince decided to marry her.

The princess was very picky about peas, wasn't she? Help her decide what kind of dinner to serve at her birthday party. Here is a list of the foods she does NOT like:

✗ green vegetables
✗ anything round
✗ any foods that have cheese in them

Circle the foods on the list below that will make the princess happy.

roast beef
whole cranberries
corn
hot rolls and butter
creamed chicken
mashed potatoes with cheese sauce
carrots and celery
banana bread and butter

8

ATTRIBUTES

Proper Dress Required

The princess is also picky about what people should wear to her party. Here are the kinds of clothes she likes:

* long dresses
* hats with bows
* gloves
* short sleeves
* high heels

Each of the guests must have at least three of these things to wear to the party. Circle the ladies who were invited.

SEQUENCING, LOGICAL REASONING

So Little Time! So Much to Do!

It's almost time for the party! The servants have a list of the chores that need to be done, but they're not sure what to do first. There are also some things on the list that don't belong.

Help the servants by numbering the steps in the order you think they belong. Cross out the chores that don't need to be done. (Remember, there may be more than one way to do things!)

- cook the food
- clean the ballroom floor
- play kickball
- find out how many guests are coming
- set the tables
- paint pictures
- set up the tables and chairs
- buy the food
- collect seashells

CREATIVE WRITING

An Event to Remember

Pretend that you are a newspaper reporter who just attended the wedding of the picky princess and the handsome prince. Write a newspaper story about the wedding. Then draw some pictures to go with the story.

The Times

The Wedding of the Year!!

The Royal couple.

Loyal subjects celebrate.

CLASSIFICATION/LOGICAL REASONING

Where Does It Belong?

Fill in the Category Chart below. Look at the categories listed across the top. Then fill in the boxes with words that fit each of the categories AND begin with one of the letters to the left of the chart.

	Animals	Foods	Places	Things To Do
M	monkey			
B		banana		
P				play piano
S			school	

Create-a-Chart

Make up a Category Chart of your own. Choose your own categories and your own alphabet letters. If you and a friend each make a chart, you can play this game together. Whoever fills in the other's chart first wins the game!

CREATIVE WRITING

Silly Sentences

Make up silly sentences using each of the category words you listed for some of the alphabet letters! Draw pictures to go with them.

A polar bear ate peanuts and played the piano in the park.

Then make up silly sentences another way. Open a book and turn to a page. Close your eyes and point to a word. Do this 3 times. Then use the 3 words in a silly sentence.

CLASSIFICATION/LOGICAL REASONING

What Do We Have in Common?

Look at each picture. Think of 3 things that are like the object in the picture in some way. Write the 3 things on the lines provided next to the picture. Then tell WHY they are alike.

1. bathtub—both hold liquid
2. plate—both used for meals
3. cookie—both begin with "c"

15

CLASSIFICATION/LOGICAL REASONING

A Fitting Place

The figure below is called a Venn Diagram. It is used to explain things and to solve problems in many different ways.

Each one of the pictures below can fit into one of the spaces in the Venn diagram. Draw the pictures or write the words in the numbered spaces. Each picture will be used only once.

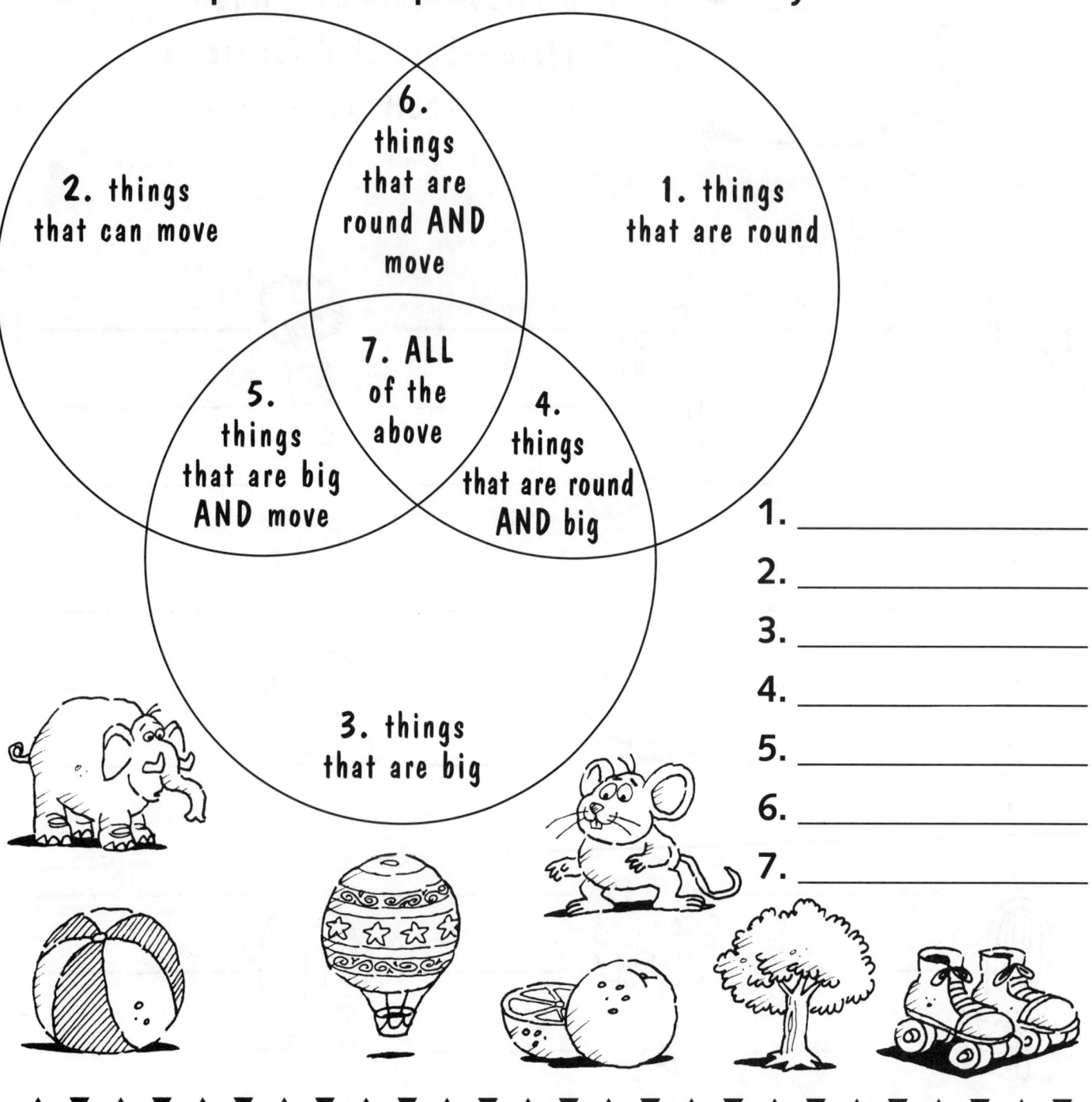

1. _____
2. _____
3. _____
4. _____
5. _____
6. _____
7. _____

ATTRIBUTES/CREATIVE THINKING

Flags of Fancy

Did you know that everything on a flag stands for something? The 13 stripes on the American flag stand for the original 13 colonies, and the stars stand for the 50 states. The red maple leaf on the Canadian flag is symbolic of the maple tree, which is common to Canada.

Other colors, shapes, and symbols have meaning, too.

yellow—strong
green—alive
purple—royal
orange—fire
brown—earth
black—proud
owl—smart

circle—never ending
triangle—together
rectangle—safe
diamond—rich
bear—big, strong
bird—free
lion—king

Design your own flag on a separate piece of paper. Tell a story about you and your family using the symbols above. You may make up some symbols of your own, too.

LOGICAL REASONING

The Bone Zone

Brittany and Josh went to a museum. They wanted to know about a big skeleton they saw there. Help them find out about the skeleton by writing some questions.

What _____ ????
Where _____ ????
When _____ ????
How _____ ????
Why _____ ????
Who _____ ????

FOLLOWING DIRECTIONS

Creature Features

When Brittany and Josh found out what the skeleton was, they were amazed! Draw a creature that might have lived a long time ago. Follow the directions below.

Follow these directions:
1. The creature is very tall.
2. It stands on two feet.
3. The creature has a long tail.
4. The front feet are very short.
5. The creature has sharp claws.
6. Its head is long and pointed.
7. Its mouth is full of sharp teeth!

What do you think the creature is? Can you give it a name?

ATTRIBUTES/LOGICAL REASONING

Pen Pal Partners

A teacher has collected some letters from children who want to be friends with children in other places.

Dear Pen Pal,

I am 7 years old. I love school. I like to play games on my computer. I like to read.
Your friend,
Brandon

Dear Friend,

I will be in grade 3 next year. I love to fish and ride horses. I have a twin brother. We build things together.

Your pal,
Eric

Dear Pen Pal,
My favorite thing to do is look at books. My mom works in a library and I spend all day there when I'm not in school. Sometimes I get to play on the computer. I would like to write letters to friends all over.
Your friend,
Tiffany

Dear Pen Pal,
I'm writing this letter to you from my tree house. I built it myself (with my dad's help!). I love to be outdoors. I love animals, too. Write back soon.
From Barbara

CREATIVE WRITING

All About Me!

Would you like a pen pal? You can ask people at the library how to get a pen pal in another part of the country or even another part of the world!

✎ Write a letter introducing yourself to a person you've never met. Tell the person what you like to do, how old you are, what your family is like, and other important things in your life.

Dear Pen Pal,

Your Friend,

PROBLEM SOLVING/LOGICAL REASONING

Animal Antics

Even animals have problems! Look at these letters to Aunt Henrietta. Then look at the animals in the picture on page 23. Can you find which animals wrote the letters? Put a circle around them. Then help Aunt Henrietta solve their problems by writing on the lines below.

Dear Aunt Henrietta,
The ground where I sleep is cold and hard. I want a soft bed.
Signed,
Uncomfortable

Dear Aunt Henrietta,
I have no friends. I live all alone. Please help!
Signed,
Lonely

Dear Aunt Henrietta,
I am always hungry. There is never enough food for me. All my brothers and sisters get more food than me.
Signed,
Starving

Dear Starving,

Dear Lonely,

Dear Uncomfortable,

PROBLEM SOLVING/LOGICAL REASONING

23

PROCESS OF ELIMINATION/LOGICAL REASONING

Help this boy write his name on the name tag. Cross out all the letters that come after N in the alphabet. Then write the letters that are left in order to find out the boy's name.

CREATIVE WRITING

Treasure Hunt

Imagine that you found an old treasure box! What would be inside? What would you do with the treasure?

Write a story about your treasure hunt. Draw a picture to go with the story.

LOGICAL REASONING

Animal Inventors

Did you ever wonder how some everyday things were invented? Sometimes when people look at the world around them, they see a better way to do things. Can you match the objects below with the animals that might have helped invent them?

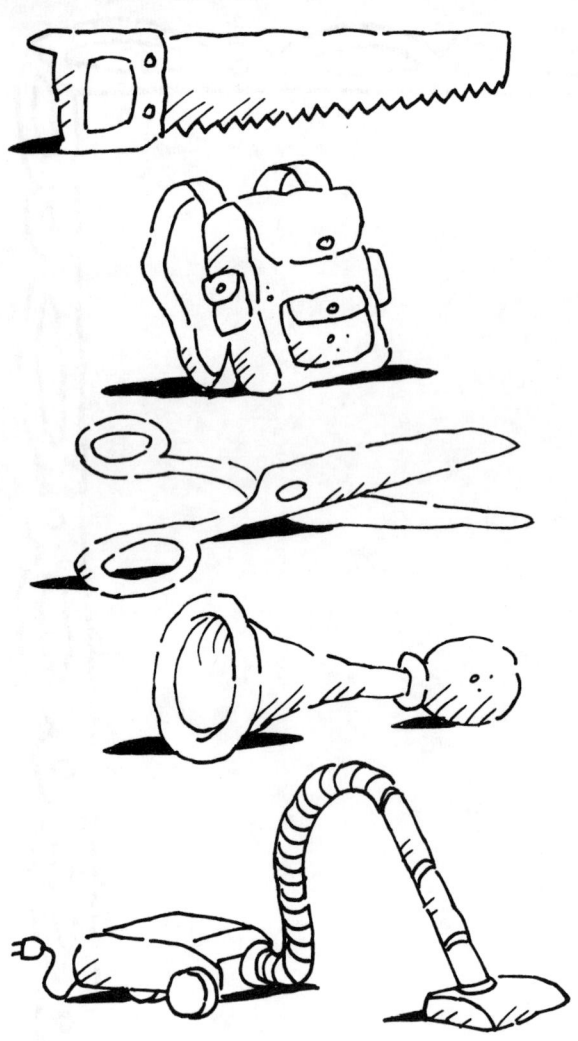

Can you think of any other animals who might have helped to invent things?

CREATIVE WRITING

Time to Clean My Room!

Suppose you could use any materials you wanted to invent a room-cleaning machine. What would you use? Draw a picture of your invention. Then write about how it works.

CREATIVE WRITING/LOGICAL REASONING

That's What You Think!

What does the world look like from another creature's eyes? Write what you think the creatures pictured below might say.

DECODING/LETTER SKILLS

Fortune Telling

Follow these directions to find your fortune.

1. Choose a number from 1 to 4.
2. Look for the squares with your number in them.
3. On another piece of paper, write the words in the order you find them.

4 YOU	1 SOON	2 YOU	3 GOOD
3 NEWS	2 WILL	4 WILL	1 YOU
4 BE	2 GET	3 WILL	1 WILL
1 BE	2 A	4 VERY	3 COME
2 SURPRISE	3 SOON	1 LUCKY	4 HAPPY

Answers:

page 3

page 4
"This is fun!"

page 5
Caption 1: May I have a job?
Caption 2: You will get a bang out of this job.
Caption 3: Does this mean I am fired?

page 8
roast beef, corn, hot rolls and butter, creamed chicken, banana bread and butter.

page 9

page 10
Answers may vary. For example:
6 or 3 - cook the food
1 or 4 - clean the ballroom floor
cross out - play kickball
2 or 1 - find out how many guests are coming
4 or 6 - set the tables
cross out - paint pictures
3 or 5 - set up the tables and chairs
5 or 2 - buy the food
cross out - collect seashells

page 16
Answers may vary. For example:
elephant (space 5), orange (space 1), beach ball (space 4), mouse (space 2), hot-air balloon (space 7), tree (space 3), roller skates (space 6).

page 22
Starving - pig
Lonely - cow
Uncomfortable - horse

page 24
Benjamin

page 26
Alex went to the park.

page 31
1. Soon you will be lucky.
2. You will get a surprise.
3. Good news will come soon.
4. You will be very happy.